TUMMIES on the run

All royalties are being donated to the
Memorial Park Conservancy

First edition

ISBN 978-1-60898-134-2 (pbk. : alk. paper)

For information about customizing *Tummies on the Run*
for your organization, please contact
tummies@namelos.com

Memorial Park Conservancy, Inc.
6501 Memorial Drive
Houston, Texas 77007-7021

Tummies on the run

Andrea White & Mimi Vance

ILLUSTRATIONS BY

Rob Shepperson

Rhyming on the Run

Houston, Texas

Big Red Jogger, here we go!
My Pop behind and Spot below.

Park – Memorial Park – hooray!
My tummy wants to run today.

Tummies round and flat and fun,
A world of tummies on the run.

Tummies short and tummies tall,
And some, like mine, are kind of small.

Hot or cold or wet or dry,
Some tummies dance, some tummies sigh.

Jiggles, shimmies, hops, and shakes,
So many moves a tummy makes.

Some just walk, some jog or fly.
Did that sweet Grandma pass us by?

Faster tummies huff and puff
And slower tummies say ENOUGH!

Tummies frown, but Pop just smiles.
My tummy bounces all those miles!

Jelly Belly, hold on tight!
We swerve around a doggy fight.

Round Memorial Park we go,
And when we'll stop, I just don't know.

Come on, Houston, this is fun!
It's time for tummies on the run.

Saggy tummies, hanging low
As Labs and Poodles say hello.

Tummies arching in the air,
That white one has such curly hair.

Frisbees, bikers, golfers, kites,
Memorial Park is full of sights.

Tummies round and flat and fun,
It's furry tummies on the run.

Some run quickly, some relax.
Two big ones roll to scratch their backs.

Yorkies low, Great Danes up high.
Is that a Sheepdog racing by?

Water fountain! Now we stop
So Pop can slurp and Spot can plop.

Tongues a-slobber, barking loud –
Look out! Here comes the Beagle crowd.

Ears are drooping in the bowl.
Heads low and wet, the droplets roll.

Sloppy water sloshes round.
Their drinking makes a silly sound.

Tummies resting, bunching, talk.
The Beagles take a vote: "Let's walk."

Pop says, "Time to leave the park."
The sun has set. It's almost dark.

Hurry, Pop, now move those feet.
My tummy's tired! It's time to eat!

Tummies hurry, scurry so
All day and night – Why? I don't know!

Spot's and Pop's and mine all do,
So get your tummy running, too!

About Memorial Park

Memorial Park, encompassing 1,500 acres, has bike trails, tennis courts, a swimming pool, and baseball fields, but *Tummies on the Run* refers to the heart of Memorial Park, which is its 3-mile running loop. About 10,000 runners use Seymour Lieberman Exercise Trail daily. People are out at all hours, and in all weathers, running, jogging, walking. No bicycles are allowed on the running trail, although bikers zip by on the nearby street. Houston has a semitropical climate, and people work hard year-round to stay fit. Many army units, school track teams, and fitness groups train in Memorial Park alongside slower joggers.

Help us to Plan, Protect, and Preserve Memorial Park. Please become a member of the Memorial Park Conservancy and help us to support the park's jogging trail, open spaces, natural habitat, and amenities. To join, go to our website: *www.memorialparkconservancy.org*.

Andrea White, an almost lifelong Houston resident, likes to walk around Memorial Park even on the hottest days of the summer, when the tummies come out. The running trail represents to her great conversations, secrets told, problems solved, and friendships forged. She is the author of four books of historical fiction, including her latest, *Windows on the World*, about a young girl who time-travels to the Twin Towers to rescue her great-grandmother. For details, view her website: *www.upcitychronicles.com*. She and Mimi Vance, partners in rhyme, team up to produce picture books.

Mimi Brian Vance has been fortunate enough to walk in parks and on trails all around the world. Married to a native Houstonian, she now enjoys introducing her children to Houston's wonderful parks, including Memorial Park. A Louisiana-born storyteller and a former U.S. diplomat, she loves words and languages. Her passion for using American Sign Language with hearing children before they can speak inspired her to write the *Words by the Handful* series of children's board books. Her website, *www. wordsbythehandful.com*, is a rich resource for anyone wanting to sign with babies and toddlers.

Illustrator **Rob Shepperson** lives and works in Croton-on-Hudson, New York. *www.robshepperson.com*.

CPSIA information can be obtained
at www.ICGtesting.com
Printed in the USA
LVIW021914280412

279426LV00002B